CUBBY'S WORLD
Story of a Baby Bear

CUBBY'S WORLD

Story of a Baby Bear
by Robbie Trent

illustrated by Margo Locke

Nashville   ABINGDON PRESS   New York

ISBN 0-687-10054-2
Library of Congress Catalog Card Number: 66-16997

To
children everywhere
who can understand
a baby bear
and what he found
out about the world

Far back in the deep woods, the limbs of a large tree stretched gray among the green cedars.

Once that tree, too, had been green, but now the leaves were gone, and the tree was dead.

Low, near the ground, a black hole opened into the hollow trunk of the tree. Inside the hole a mother bear and her two babies lay on a nest of grass and leaves.

7

Slowly the smallest bear uncurled himself and stretched until his body was almost as long as your hand. He reached out a tiny paw and felt the warmth of his mother. His mouth nuzzled her and found the softness of her breast. His lips moved in the softness, and he felt warm milk in his mouth. He swallowed and nuzzled his mother again and again. The warm milk felt good in his throat and filled his stomach until it was round and full. Then Cubby went to sleep.

For days he awoke only when he was hungry. And always he felt the softness and nuzzled his mother until he found the warm milk and drank until he was full.

"The world is soft," Cubby decided.

8

When he was a month old, Cubby opened his eyes for the first time and saw the darkness. He saw one large lump of darkness which he knew was his mother. And he saw something else.

He saw beside him a lump of darkness, smaller than his mother but larger than himself, a lump of darkness a little longer than your hand.

Cubby put out his paw and touched the lump. It was warm and soft and slick. The lump moved, and Cubby knew that it was his brother. He licked him with his wet tongue. He and his brother nuzzled their mother and swallowed the warm milk until their stomachs were full. Then they closed their eyes in the darkness.

"All the world is dark," Cubby decided as he went to sleep.

Days passed. The two cubs grew stronger and longer. They slept most of the time.

When they were two months old, springtime came. The baby bears discovered something hard and sharp in their mouths. Their teeth were coming in.

One day their mother stirred and yawned. She grunted to tell her sons that it was time to leave the den in the old tree. At last they could go out into the woods.

Cubby and his brother followed their mother as she crawled out of the tree.

Outside the tree they stood quite still for a moment. They blinked their eyes. The darkness was gone.

The sun was shining. There was light!

Cubby saw that his mother was not a great lump of darkness but a furry animal with four short legs. He looked at his brother and saw a slick little animal, not so black as himself, with a little spot on his nose.

The two little bears followed their mother down to a clear stream of water. When Cubby looked down into the water, he saw that he was almost as big as his brother, and he seemed blacker than his brother. He was deep black like his mother. He was as black as the deep, deep darkness he had left in the hollow tree.

Cubby reached out his paw and touched the wetness of the water. He put down his head and drank.

Then he and his brother followed

their mother back into the woods.

"We must find food for you to eat," the mother bear told the cubs. "You must learn which grasses and nuts are best. You must find acorns and berries to eat. Sometimes you can find sweet-tasting honey."

18

She pushed away the dead leaves, and the three bears ate the tender young grass that was beginning to grow. They found nuts and ants. Later they found berries just turning red. They found raspberries and huckleberries, blackberries and strawberries.

19

All day they ran through the woods in the sunshine.

"The world is light," Cubby decided.

But when nighttime came and the light went away, he wondered if it would come back.

When Cubby opened his eyes the next morning, he saw the sun.

Every night the darkness came, and every morning the light came.

One morning Cubby opened his eyes very, very early and saw the darkness fade into grayness and the grayness change to pink. He watched the pinkness turn into light when the sun climbed higher in the sky.

"The world is light, and the world is dark," Cubby decided.

20

One day the bears found a beehive. The mother showed the little bears how to break it and tear the hardness away. The three scooped out the honey with their paws. Cubby dug in both paws and licked the sweetness from them. He dug deeper and a bee stung him on his tender nose. He jumped up and down in pain.

"The world is not all soft," Cubby decided. "Some of it stings and hurts."

22

The days grew longer. The sun shone warmer. Cubby and his brother played together often in the woods. They chased each other around the trees. They scuffled and played tricks on each other, hiding in the bushes and behind the rocks. Sometimes the two little bears stood on their heads. Cubby could stand on his head a long time. Both of them turned somersaults and climbed trees.

"The world is fun," Cubby decided.

The little bears learned to swim. They learned to watch for fish in the clear water and to scoop them up with their paws.

26

They learned to run to their mother when she grunted for them to come. One day, as they played high up in a tree, she grunted for them to come down. The little bears waited a moment. She grunted again. Again Cubby and his brother waited.

Straight up the tree trunk the mother bear climbed. She gave each little bear a slap and a push. Then she turned, and the small bears followed her down the tree. They were learning to mind.

29

One day Cubby's mother led him and his brother to the edge of an open field.

"Never run into the open field," she told them. "Men shoot guns there. The guns make a great noise and a puff, and whatever is in the way of the shot is hurt. Often someone is killed. Keep to the woods, and you will be safe."

31

Each day the two little bears grew longer and heavier and stronger. When they looked at each other, they saw that the long silky hair had turned into short fur. They were beginning to look more like their mother. Each day they were growing. They were larger than the fox which sometimes ran in the woods. They were as large as the black dog which often came over the hill.

32

One day, as they played, the two little bears came near the open field.

"It would be nice to run there," the biggest one said.

Cubby shook his head.

"It is not safe to play there," he said. But when he was not looking, his brother ran out into the field.

Cubby started to run after him. Then he heard a great noise.

35

As Cubby stood still, he saw his brother stop for a moment and then fall to the ground. He did not move at all.

Cubby ran for his mother. She told him his brother was dead. "He will not come back," she said.

Cubby found that it was not so much fun playing by himself. He missed the romps with his brother. He missed having someone to tease and turn somersaults with.

36

"The world is sad," Cubby decided.

Yet, as the days went by, he learned to enjoy the warm sunshine again even when he played by himself. And he was always glad for the light.

Cubby grew fatter and fatter as winter came. His fur grew thicker and thicker. Instead of the half a pound he had weighed when he was born, he now weighed forty pounds.

The days grew shorter. The sun did not shine high over Cubby's head as long as it had in the summertime. Its light was not so bright, and the days were not so warm.

39

Each day Cubby watched the sun go down earlier. He saw the soft light fade away into darkness. Each night the darkness came earlier and lasted longer.

"Soon it will be time," Cubby heard his mother say one day.

He came closer and listened.

40

"Soon it will be time to go into the den for winter."

Slowly Cubby asked a question. "Will we go back into the darkness?"

"Yes," replied his mother. "The darkness is good for sleeping and for resting. It is the way of bears to sleep most of the winter in darkness. We will walk in the light again when spring comes."

"I like the light," Cubby said. "I do not want to go back into the darkness."

His mother walked away.

42

The wind blew colder and colder. Ice froze on the little stream of water. One morning Cubby saw something white on the top of a tall mountain. Great flakes of snow were falling. Soon all the ground was white.

Cubby felt hard bits of ice sting his nose. He shivered.

"It is time now," his mother said.

She walked away toward the hollow tree deep in the woods.

44

Cubby stood quite still for a moment. He looked at the snow. Then he looked up at the sun.

"Good-bye, light," he whispered.

Slowly he followed his mother into the deep woods and crawled with her into the old hollow tree.

45

The darkness was even blacker than he remembered it. Cubby shut his eyes and thought.

Cubby thought of the sunny days when he had played in the woods. He opened his eyes.

Suddenly he decided something. The darkness was not everywhere. He could remember light. If he shut his eyes very tight, he could almost see it!

"We will walk in the light again when spring comes."

Cubby stretched himself as far as he could. He felt his mother's warm body, and he curled into a ball.

"It is the way of bears to sleep the winter in darkness," he whispered to himself,

46

but before he went to sleep, he had a big thought:

In the world there is softness like my mother,
And there is hardness like ice.
There is warmness like summer,
And there is coldness like winter.
In the world there is fun,
And there is sadness.
The world is darkness,
And the world is light.
But even when we see the darkness,
The light is always there.